DEEP GORGE

MOUNTAINS

BEWILDERBOAT JUNCTION

PEACEFUL PLAINS

OGGLE VILLAGE

SCARY LA

A BeWILDermuddle

Other Bewilder books

A Boggle at Bewilderwood
The Bewilderbats

Jermuddle

TOM BLOFELD

Illustrated by
STEVE PEARCE

HOLLY DAY & BUMP PUBLISHING

First published in 2010 by
Holly Day & Bump Publishing
BeWILDerwood, Horning Road, Hoveton
Norwich NR12 8JE
www.BeWILDerwood.co.uk
Reprinted 2011

ISBN 978 0 9555 433 9

A catalogue record for this book
is available from the British Library

Typeset in Great Britain by Antony Gray
Printed and Bound in China

3 4 5 6 7 8 9

To
Rufus and Eve
with bottomless love

Ticklechin's Tale

There was a great commotion in the Boggle village.

'The Grubbles are coming. The Grubbles are coming,' shouted a little Boggle boy as he ran up and down the twisting wooden bridges between the Boggle houses. He rushed past an elderly pipe-chewing Boggle struggling to find his ear trumpet.

'The Grubbles? Did you say the Grubbles?' asked the old Boggle, as he finally put his ear trumpet in the right place. But the boy didn't hear him.

'Did you say the Grubbles are on their way?' he asked again, but the small boy was already running down the spiral stairs to the main village platform. The old pipe-chewer decided to follow him, very slowly.

The Boggle village was built deep in the marshes, right next to the pongy ponds where the Boggles did their fishing. All their houses were built high up in the bulrushes and were joined by a maze of walkways and platforms. In the middle of the village was the largest platform, where the villagers met to have big discussions or feasts. It was decorated with hanging baskets full of lovely blue flowers. At one end was a stage for Boggle singing and, at the other, a chair was reserved for the most elderly and venerable of the Boggles.

The old Boggle, whose name was Ticklechin, finally reached the chair and sat down in it very slowly. He could see a small crowd of children who had gathered about to hear the news.

'But who are the Grubbles?' asked the smallest Boggle. All the children started talking at once, but nobody seemed to know very much.

Then Ticklechin cleared his throat loudly and everyone turned to look at him.

'You want to hear about the Grubbles do you? I'll tell you a tale about Grubbles if you like,' he said. 'They're good friends to the Boggles, they are. But before I can tell you, could one of you little ones run over to my hut and fetch me my pair of old socks?'

It seemed an odd request, but Boggle children mostly do what they are asked. So a swarm of young Boggles ran over to the old creaky hut on the edge of the village where Ticklechin lived.

After some rummaging about, because the old Boggle was a bit messy, they found a very old pair of socks. They were a rather dingy colour of pinkie-grey and were made of a lot of holes held together with not very much sock. Two small Boggles brought them back to the village platform, holding each sock at arm's length using just one finger and a thumb.

Old Ticklechin was very pleased to see them.

'My old pair of socks. Soon they'll be as good as new. I've had these since I was knee-high to a slitherigrub.' He sat up in the chair reserved for the most eminent and elderly villagers and draped the socks over his knees.

'So you want to know who the Grubbles are,' he asked the

group of little Boggles sitting around him. Everybody did. He adjusted his ear trumpet and leaned forward.

'Well . . . nobody knows where they come from except, I suppose, the Grubbles themselves. Yes, I feel sure they would know that.' He rubbed his chin thoughtfully and went very quiet as he pondered this.

'Don't forget about the story,' reminded a little Boggle cautiously.

'Ah yes ... the story, the story. Well, I'll tell you all about it,' he said, leaning back in his chair.

'A long time ago, when I was a young Boggle, my mum sent me out to gather berries. It was a terrible year for berries and all the crows had eaten what there was. So I had to go further than I ever had before. I went all the way to the Dismal Dyke, but still there weren't any berries at all. So I pushed my boat to a place I'd only heard about. We call it the Long Lagoon and it's a very long way away indeed.'

There were admiring gasps from the listening children. Boggles aren't very brave and going all the way to the Long Lagoon seemed to them like a really big adventure.

'Well, I was glad I did as there were some lovely berries there - plenty of them. I was filling my basket when I heard what sounded like music. It was such pretty music, made by flutes and lyres and things like that.'

Ticklechin cocked his head silently as though he could hear them again now.

The Boggle children waited patiently and, after a while, he continued: 'Then, I saw some smoke rising softly from the reeds at the far end of the lagoon. I thought it might be someone cooking and as it had been a long boat trip, and I didn't want to eat any berries because they were for the feast, I had a careful look at who was making the fire and if they might have a little bite for me.

'And then I saw them. There were lots of nice, round, cosy sort of people, all sitting about a camp-fire listening to songs and knitting. Every now and then they would take what they were knitting and put it in a big cauldron. And when they took the knitting out again it was a beautiful colour of red.

'Well, it seemed best that I just slip away as I couldn't eat knitting you know, but as I began to go, one of them saw me and called me back. They seemed very friendly, so I went over and said hello.'

Ticklechin leaned forward and dropped his voice to a whisper, as though he was telling them a big secret.

'What they were was a tribe of travelling Grubbles, and I'd found them.' He sat back and looked terribly proud to have been so intrepid.

Then he stroked his old socks again and carried on with his tale.

'They said that Grubbles didn't live in villages like we do, but went from place to place, sleeping in tents that they carried on their backs. They spent their time finding berries and roots to dye their clothes. They wore such lovely clothes – every sort of bright colours they were – and with spangly, shiny jewels on all their hats. They told me that the Long Lagoon was the only place to find a special little berry which was the best one for making red dye. So they had come there to pick some.

'They only used red for dying their socks though. I think

they thought they looked nicer that way. So, quick as a flash, I pulled off my boots and asked if they would dye my socks too. They looked at them and said that they would have to mend them first. Next, they asked me if I'd like something to eat while I was waiting for the socks to be darned.

'Of course I said, "Yes please," immediately. But when I saw what they ate I wasn't so sure. It was a kind of sludgy green slush which they called pongiporridge. It was the only thing they ate. Well, it wouldn't do to refuse a kindness so I had to eat it too.'

Old Ticklechin grimaced at the memory. 'Have any of you little knee-highs had to eat mud stew?'

'*Yeuch!* Horrible!' they all cried in unison.

'Well, it's delicious compared to pongiporridge. It tastes like

this.' Ticklechin stuck out his tongue and pulled on it with both hands, making a very sour face at the same time. The Boggle children laughed loudly and some of them started pulling on their tongues as well.

'Still, the Grubbles like it and that's what counts, I reckon. Anyway, I thought that it would be nice to ask them to our feast and then they could try Boggle food instead. So they all came, and that's how the Grubbles and the Boggles became friends. If I remember, they ate a great deal of sweetsludge pie, though.

'And these,' Ticklechin concluded, holding up his battered pair of socks, 'are the very socks they dyed for me. I do hope they can mend them again.'

Then he looked down at his gaggle of listeners.

'That's enough dawdling, little Boggles. If you want to know any more, you'll have to ask Oakum in the Twiggle village. He knows lots about Grubble ways, you know. But you'd better be off, helping with the party we'll throw for them when they get here. Off you go.'

The children all thanked Ticklechin for his story and ran off to collect nuts and fruit. They left the ancient Boggle rocking in his chair, fondly stroking his old socks.

They were all very excited as there was to be another party.

The Soulful Song

Today was another warm hazy kind of day in Bewilderwood, just the sort of day when everything seems to be a little stiller than usual. An odd butterfly flapped lazily in the air and the reeds hardly rustled.

Down on the Boggle village jetty, where they kept their fishing boats, the wise Witch of Bewilderwood was talking to

the Boggles. She was a very nice witch, if you were a nice Boggle, and she protected all the creatures in the woods. She was discussing the coming of the Grubbles.

'You ought to decide on someone to go and ask the Grubbles to the party,' she suggested.

'Couldn't you go?' asked a pretty Boggle called Marsha. 'You were the one who found them this time, and you also know the way.'

'I'd love to,' the witch said, 'but I have lots of things to do before the party. In any case, it would be nicer if one of you invited them yourselves.'

The truth is that Boggles don't really like big adventures. They much prefer being at home, eating lots of yummy food. A Boggle adventure mostly consists of going to the pongy ponds, with a small snack, to do some fishing.

'Ticklechin knows the way. Perhaps he should go,' suggested someone.

'I'm not sure if I'm quite as young as I was, you know,' said Ticklechin, shaking his head sadly. Then he brightened up.

'Perhaps Swampy should go. He's done the most travelling of all of us. He can take my socks along with him for the Grubbles to mend. They love mending things.'

Everyone except Swampy agreed enthusiastically.

Swampy never used to be a good traveller, but he had been on two big adventures before and was getting a little better at them now. Even so, Boggles aren't keen on exploring alone and Swampy decided he would go over to the Twiggle village in the woods to ask Moss and Leaflette to join him.

Moss was his cousin and had married a pretty Twiggle called

Leaflette. They lived in the Twiggle village, high up in the trees. The three of them had been on journeys together before.

Twiggles are relatives of Boggles and they get along with them very well. They love dancing and climbing and are very elegant. They also cook scrumptious things like barkicrisps and nutbug cluster. At least Swampy was looking forward to that bit of the journey.

Just the same, Swampy packed some food as it was never sensible to go travelling without a little snack to help you along the way. He was in his house, wrapping the sweetsludge pie in leaves to keep it safe and cutting a slice of sedgepuff cake, when the witch came by to ask if she could travel with him because she was heading that way anyway. Swampy was very pleased to have her for the company, and he always felt safer with the witch by his side. Soon, they both set off for the high trees of Bewilderwood.

When they got to the Twiggle village, it turned out that Leaflette had far too much washing to do in preparation for the party, so she couldn't come. But Moss said he would go with Swampy, if the witch thought it was not too dangerous, and the witch proposed that Oakum should go along too. Oakum actually seemed pleased to join them.

'Why not ask Mildred to take you there,' the witch suggested. 'She knows the way because that's where she takes her annual mud bath.'

This seemed a very good idea. Mildred was an enormous thorny crocklebog and could take everyone there on her back. She looked quite frightening with all her scary teeth, but Swampy knew that she was very friendly, and a vegetarian.

Boggles are always afraid of being eaten up by bigger animals so they are especially keen on all large animals becoming vegetarians.

So, after they had shared all of Leaflette's nutbug crunch and drank a big fizzy glass of acorn beer, they were ready to set off. They all knew the way to the Scary Lake where Mildred spent her time, so after tying their snack bundles up, Swampy, Oakum and Moss set off on their way through the woods.

Travelling Boggles and Twiggles love to sing. At first they sang Boggle songs, because Moss and Swampy were Boggles. These songs are all rather loud with very noisy choruses and there is a lot of foot stomping and back-slapping involved. After a while, Oakum sang them a few Twiggle tunes, which are much prettier and full of sunshine.

'I know another kind of song I could sing, if you like,' said Oakum. The others said that they would like that very much.

Oakum started singing a slow, mournful melody, which seemed to fill the woods with a sad, yet beautiful air. It seemed that even the squirrels were stopping their scampering and sitting still to listen. The song grew more beautiful and haunting and it made them feel that everything around them was perfect. The yellow flowers were swaying as if in time, and the purple butterflies were all stretching their wings out gently in the dappled sunshine.

When Oakum had finished, Swampy was silent for a little while and then he whispered quietly to Moss: 'That was the loveliest song that I've ever heard.'

They wondered where Oakum had learned it, but they were feeling so peaceful that they didn't ask. They strode along in silence for a while and it wasn't long before they had travelled through the dark tunnel which led to the Deep Reeds, and onwards through the marshes to the Scary Lake.

At the lake's edge they looked, but there was no Mildred. The coots were dabbling happily and a few ducks were quacking gently by the overhanging branches. But there was not a large crocklebog in sight.

'Well, I suppose it couldn't hurt to have a small nibble while we wait and see if she comes back,' suggested Moss. So they did just that.

After a little while, Swampy suggested they might have another bite or two as it was never good to feel peckish. But just as he was about to take a huge piece of sedgepuff cake there was a sort of watery explosion right beside him. He jumped out of the way as fast as he could and just avoided being drenched. But the piece of cake was completely soaked with muddy water.

From under the nearest branch emerged the most enormous toothy grin of Mildred the Crocklebog.

'Hello everyone,' she said gaily, in her excitable lisp, 'It'*th* me again. I didn't get you wet did I? Only I *th*ometimes breathe water in*th*ead of air when I'm happy to meet people and it com*th* out of my no*th*e.'

Swampy looked rather mournfully at the sedgepuff cake. You could eat it when it was soggy, but it was much nicer when it wasn't.

'We're fine, Mildred,' said Moss. 'We're getting used to you now and nobody got wet this time. We were calling to you, only you didn't hear us.'

'I wa*th* underwater, learning to hold my breath. I'm trying out *th*ynchroni*th*ed *th*wimming.'

'That's nice,' said Swampy. 'Who are you doing it with?'

'Ju*th*t me,' said Mildred brightly. 'There aren't any other thorny crocklebog*th* here to join in.'

Swampy offered Mildred his soggy cake to eat while they explained why they had come to see her. She agreed to come along straight away, although they had to wait a few moments while she collected her soap and loofah because, Mildred said very sensibly, that she could have a bath at the same time, and then that would be over for another year.

They all set off on Mildred's back to find the Grubbles.

The Grubble Greeting

Although it was quite a long way to the marshy spot where the Grubbles had chosen to set up their camp, it was an easy journey. They passed bright green reeds and lots of the beautiful yellow flowers which decorate the marshes so perfectly in early summer. The happy buzz of tiny insects could be heard, as they rushed from flower to flower as if delighted that spring had finally come to an end. A little kingfisher sat on the end of Mildred's swishy tail to enjoy the ride for some of the way. Even the Dismal Dyke seemed a bit less gloomy than usual.

There was a little bit of trouble, just before they arrived at the Long Lagoon, because Mildred squeezed her soap too hard and it shot off into the muddy water. They tried to look for it, but it was lost in the mud.

Eventually Mildred announced: 'Never mind about the *th*oap. The really important thing i*th* to have heap*th* of mud. And I've got my loofah to help clean up after.'

So they carried on.

As they eased their way into the Long Lagoon, the sun came bursting out from behind a cloud. Everywhere were birds, chattering in the warm air. Nearby was a little black coot snuffling in the grassy bank, and it came over to see the strange

sight of Mildred with her passengers. It chirruped a happy hello. Mildred was delighted.

'I've tried to be friend*th* with a coot for year*th* now. That'*th* the only one who ever *th*aid hello!'

Huge spouts of water came shooting from her nose as she explained this to the others, but she didn't splash anyone, not even the coot.

They offered the little bird some crumbs of seedibuns and it flustered around them contentedly as they made their way across the huge expanse of water.

Then Oakum shouted out: 'Look. It's the Grubbles. They're over there!'

At the far corner of the lake were wisps of smoke and brown tent tops, just visible above the reeds. Oakum waved his hat in the air to attract the Grubbles' attention. From the commotion in the reeds, they could tell that they had been spotted.

The Grubbles seemed a bit unsure about what to do when they saw Mildred, with all her teeth and spines. But one of them called out: 'That's Oakum riding on its back. He's come to see us! That means the creature he's riding must be friendly.'

The next moment, lots of tiny boats, which the Grubbles called coracles, were being launched as they all set off into the water to greet the group of travellers. The boats were only big enough for one or two Grubbles each, and were made of brown canvas. Soon, a bobbing fleet of paddling Grubbles were steering noisily towards them. Everyone seemed very excited as they all drew near.

The Grubbles who were the nearest started shouting.

'Oakum! It's Oakum!' they called.

Oakum waved back with his hat.

'Hello, everyone. I'm back. How nice to see everyone!' he called out happily.

'Hello Oakum, how lovely to see you again. Your mum and dad will be so pleased you've come back,' said a smiling Grubble in the nearest coracle. He pulled up to Mildred and introduced himself as Coney.

Oakum hugged Coney, which isn't easy in a coracle. Then he laughed and clapped his hands with joy at the prospect of seeing his parents. The others had to hold onto him quite hard to be sure that nobody fell off Mildred in all the excitement.

'I didn't know that your parents lived with the Grubbles,' Swampy said to Oakum. 'So that was why you wanted to come along.'

'I was hoping they'd be here,' said Oakum happily. 'They used to live with me in the trees, because my mum is a Twiggle,

21

but my dad's a Grubble and he missed the travelling so much that when I was old enough to get my own house, they both went back to live with the Grubbles. I liked being with the Twiggles, so I stayed in the woods, but I often miss them. It will be so wonderful to see them again.'

Mildred was surrounded by more smiling, chattering Grubbles, who guided them all back to their camp. Mildred explained to a few of them who she was and although they were pleased to meet her, they paddled their little boats a bit further away in case she sank them. Nonetheless, everyone got to the reeds safely and Moss, Swampy and Oakum clambered onto dry land.

Swampy rubbed his trouser-seat for a while because sitting on a spiny crocklebog's back for a long time can be just a little uncomfortable.

The Grubbles jumped noisily out of their tiny boats. Moss watched them as they picked up their light coracles and hoisted them onto their heads as they walked through the tall swaying reeds to the higher ground. Then he saw them remove a few bendy willow sticks from the canvas, and suddenly, the boats were folded up into little bundles and strapped onto their backs.

'That's a clever way to carry a boat about,' he said admiringly to a Grubble.

'It's not just a boat though,' replied the Grubble. 'If we push in longer willow sticks, then it becomes a tent which we can sleep in.'

The Grubble pointed at a clearing in the reeds and, sure enough, around a big warm bonfire were lots of pointed brown canvas tents. Over the nearby fire they had hung a great big steaming cauldron. Sitting next to the fire were more Grubbles, all wearing brightly coloured clothes and spangled hats.

Coney and Oakum had nearly got to the camp when Oakum's parents saw him. There were a lot of happy shouts and hugs. Oakum's mum wouldn't let go of him.

'Have you been eating enough, Oakum?' she asked, but one glance at Oakum's rather large tummy was all that was needed to suggest that he had.

The whole tribe welcomed Moss, Swampy and Mildred and everybody was introduced to everyone else. Although Mildred seemed terribly friendly, the Grubbles were quite pleased when she announced that, if nobody minded, she would slip off and have her bath while they chatted. Creatures who sneezed out water and fire didn't go all that well together, they reasoned.

'We'll take Swampy and Moss home in our boats,' said Oakum's dad, 'so you can take as long as you like in your bath. I do like a good soak myself. But before you go, you must have a nice bowl of pongiporridge. There's no point in feeling hungry right before a bath.'

A steaming bowl of something green and unusual-smelling was offered to Mildred at the lagoon's edge. She looked at it carefully and then sniffed the lazy vapour that was flowing out of the bowl and drifting downwards towards the ground.

'I think I'm not all that hungry today,' she announced. 'I'll only have one little bite.'

Mildred put a spoonful of the stuff between her jaws and poured it in. She sat up suddenly and then she pushed her jaw shut with both claws.

'*Yeauuch!*' she exclaimed and dived below the surface. Great spouts of water flew this way and that and eventually Mildred emerged making *phthooie* noises and spitting a few jets of water here, there and everywhere.

'Not good for crocklebog*th*, that *th*tuff. But thank you anyway, everybody. Well, now I've eaten I think I'll pop off for my bath.' And off she swam away, making more little spitting noises.

'I don't think she liked the pongiporridge,' said Coney to Moss. 'Not everybody does.'

'That means there's more for the rest of us,' cried out Oakum's father. 'Let's have a feast. We've just made a huge fresh pot.'

'Ah!' said Moss, with a thoughtful look on his face. 'I think I shouldn't as I'm saving myself for the big party we were going to throw for you. Oh, I forgot to ask. Can you all come?'

'We'd love to!' they all agreed in unison.

Then Swampy produced the battered old pinkie-grey socks and explained that Ticklechin was hoping the Grubbles would not mind mending them.

'Oh yes please. We love mending things. It's what Grubbles do best,' exclaimed Coney. There was quite a discussion as to who would do it, as everybody seemed to want to. Eventually, Oakum's father was given the task and he sat down by the fire to mend all the holes. His fingers seemed to be moving in a dance as he stitched each sock together.

When they were mended, he picked up a long stick with a hook on the end. He hung the socks on the hook and dipped them into the large, steaming cauldron in the middle of the fire. Swampy was very surprised.

'Do you always dip your socks in hot pongiporridge?' he asked Coney.

'Oh no!' laughed Coney. 'We eat our pongiporridge cold. That cauldron is full of red dye, which we make out of boiled grizzleberries. They make the best red colour.'

'But aren't grizzleberries terribly dangerous?' worried Swampy. 'I ate one once and had tummy-ache for a week.'

'Well, we don't usually eat our socks,' laughed Coney. 'But we have some magic powder we sprinkle over the dye at the end, which makes it safe anyway. That's why we don't come here very often, because we have to make the powder first, from some very rare orange flowers which grow a long, long way from here.'

Oakum's father took out the socks and hung them to dry by the fire. He opened a small leather pouch and sprinkled some sparkling white dust on them. The dust seemed to fizz as it fell, and when it touched the socks, they went an even brighter red than before.

'All done!' he announced and held up two colourful, good-as-new socks for them to give back to Ticklechin.

Moss and Swampy said they had better be off as there was a lot to prepare for the big party later that night.

'Why don't we all go to the Boggle village to see if there are any more socks which need doing?' suggested Oakum's mum. 'We could help with the work too.'

Everyone thought this was a very good idea, so they picked up their tents, folding the pointy tops to one side. With a couple of willow sticks pushed into special places the tents soon become lots of little coracles.

Swampy thought the Grubbles were most ingenious.

They went off in a great group with Swampy and Coney in the leading boat. Moss was in Oakum's father's little craft, and he looked quite nervous about it turning over. Oakum's father explained that Moss just had to sit quite still and he would do all the paddling. So the great convoy all bobbed along to the end of the Long Lagoon and turned off into the Dismal Dyke. Oakum and his mother were the last to leave the Long Lagoon, because they were chatting so much about all that had happened since they last saw each other that they weren't paddling very fast.

Mildred's Mud-Bath

Mildred was enjoying her bath immensely. It mostly involved galumphing about in very thick and slimy mud, making occasional rubs with her loofah. This year Mildred also practiced her synchronised swimming moves, so it was even better fun. She even sang a song, but she could only remember the first line and a bit of the chorus, so she sang those over and over again. She sang especially loudly as she did the bits under her arms. Eventually, though, it was time to get back home.

When Mildred returned home, she was surprised to find that everyone had gone. But she remembered that Moss and Swampy had agreed to go back with the others, so she didn't worry too much. Also, she could use the nice fire the Grubbles had left behind to dry herself by. Soon she was stretched out beside it, warming herself up. It wasn't long before she drifted off to sleep and was having a lovely dream involving handbags and swimming. In the best bit, she was awarded a prize for being the most synchronised crocklebog ever and she was flicking her tail in delight.

Suddenly she woke up. She had been enjoying the dream too much, and she really had been flicking her tail. Worse, her tail had struck the big cauldron of boiling grizzleberries right on

the side. It had flown off its stand and was now lying upside down, emptying its red gloopie contents into the muddy marsh where she had just bathed.

'Oop*th*,' she gulped, 'I'd better clean that up before anyone find*th* out.'

She rushed over to the mud and tried to put the grizzleberry juice back, but the harder she tried the less it wanted to go back in the cauldron. She scooped heaps of mud into the black pot, but more kept being left behind. Soon, there was a huge sea of pink-stained mud all around her.

'Oh dear, I can't get it all back in,' she said to herself. 'Perhap*th* I'd better go and find the Grubble*th* and tell them what ha*th* happened.'

She hoped that they wouldn't be too cross about it.

As she headed out of the lagoon, back to the village, she passed the little coot she had played with before. But this time it took one look at her and scuttled noisily under some bushes. Mildred waved and splashed a bit to attract its attention, but it seemed frightened of something.

She continued wearily onwards down the Dismal Dyke.

The Pink Problem

There was a good deal of cheering when the fleet of Grubbles arrived at the Boggle village. Marsha and Swampy's mum had already made a long purple banner onto which they had stitched 'A Big Boggle Welcome to the Grubbles' in purple ribbon.

Lots of the older Boggles remembered Oakum's mum and dad from the old days.

Soon the village platform was full of noisy voices, as they remembered all the fun they used to have together. Some of the smaller Boggles ran over to the Twiggle village to let all the Twiggles know that the Grubbles had arrived.

When the dance was over, everyone applauded. Coney nudged Swampy.

'Isn't that old Ticklechin over there,' he said. 'We'd better give those socks back to him.' Ticklechin was still sitting in the chair reserved for venerable old Boggles, resting his chin on top of a walking stick. His eyes lit up when he saw the socks.

'Are those really my socks? They are as good as new. You Grubbles are so clever. Thank you. Thank you. I hope it wasn't too much trouble.' Ticklechin shook Oakum's dad's hand gratefully for a long, long time. 'I love mending socks,' explained the Grubble. 'I'll be happy to do some more if you find any.'

The old Boggle put the red woollen socks on his lap and began explaining how he was the very first in the village ever to have smart red socks dyed by the Grubbles.

'After a while, lots of us had them. It became quite the fashion. But mine were first,' he informed a group of smaller Boggles. Then he leaned back and, with a dreamy expression on his face, began to stroke the socks like they were a furry pet.

All around him were busy hands working. Some were making the bright bunting for decorating the village. Some were stirring pots out of which came the most wonderful smells imaginable. Some were laying the long communal tables with wooden spoons and bowls. And some were still chatting about the good old days when the Grubbles were last here visiting.

Soon, the Twiggles came. When they arrived there was even more whooping and cheering, and a few of the Twiggles did their famous homecoming dance, trailing little gold and silver chiffon ribbons and sprinkling flowers, as they sprang delicately about the trees.

When it was over, the Grubbles all clapped.

'We'll sing a song about that wonderful dancing, later on,' they promised.

Swampy was delighted to see that Willow and her little baby, Sticklenose, had come too. Sticklenose was wriggling in Willow's arms, trying to get down so he could crawl as fast as possible over to Swampy. They had a big hug together. Willow explained that he had only been allowed to come after he had promised that he wouldn't climb any trees. The last time he had climbed a tree, it turned out that he was better at going up them than coming back down them, and he had needed to be rescued.

In a while, Willow picked him up and tucked him comfortably into a sling across her back where he couldn't cause much mischief. He could just peer over her shoulder, so Swampy played peek-a-boo games with him for a while and Sticklenose made happy gurgling noises back.

Willow began chatting to Oakum's mum about flower arranging. She was the village expert on flowers and the two of them made huge bouquets together to decorate the tables. They were just finishing the last bouquets when Sticklenose started pointing at the sky and shouting.

'Bewilderbats! Snagglefang!' he cried.

They all looked up. A huge black cloud of bats was swarming across the sky to the village. They landed upside down, under the overhanging roofs of the Boggle huts, and the biggest bat flew over to the baby Twiggle.

'Hello Sticklenose, young fellow. Good to see you again.' said the bat.

'Hello Snagglefang. Come for party?' enquired Sticklenose.

'A party. How nice. We smelt all that delicious cooking and we thought we'd nip over to see if we could get a snack. And to help out of course,' added Snagglefang quickly, after spotting Willow giving him a fierce look.

'You bats aren't allowed to eat too much before the feast begins,' she told them sternly, wagging her finger.

'We'll hardly eat anything,' Snagglefang promised.

In fact, the bats turned out to be very useful. They flew about hanging up all the gaily coloured bunting and, with their help, it was done in no time at all. Then they lent a hand finding the ingredients which the cooks might have forgotten. When everything was made, it turned out that there wasn't quite as much nutbug crunch as everyone had expected, but there was certainly enough to go round.

Then everybody laid out the food on the tables. There was a huge mudwort jelly in the middle with different layers of colour. It was nearly as tall as Swampy, and a lot more edible. All around it were bowls of barkicrisps and honeytwigs. There were plenty of sweetsludge pies, steaming cauldrons of clunk-nettle soup and there were huge jugs of acorn beer for the grown-ups and purple slozzleberry squash for the little ones.

34

'Do you think I should go back and get some pongiporridge for the feast?' Coney asked.

'I don't think so,' replied Oakum's dad. 'To tell you the truth, I don't believe Boggles really like it very much.'

Coney looked very surprised.

'But almost everybody likes pongiporridge!' he protested.

'Not Twiggles and Boggles. In fact, when I used to live here I had to eat it in a special house I built away from the village, as they don't even like the smell,' said Oakum's dad. 'But you should try a bit of sweetsludge pie. That is just as good. Almost better.'

They both had a small slice so as not to spoil their appetite. As he licked the last tiny bits off his fingers, Coney agreed that it *was* excellent.

In the middle of all this activity, nobody had noticed Ticklechin rise slowly from his chair and, after putting on his smart red socks, walk to the middle of the village platform. He banged his stick loudly on the wooden planks and everybody stopped what they were doing and looked at him.

'*Hrrhumm.* Quiet please! I have something to say.' Ticklechin announced to the quietening crowd. 'I would like to welcome the Grubbles to our humble village. I am also delighted to say that they have made up a song for the occasion which they want to sing to you all. So . . . everyone . . . a big Bewilderwood round of applause for the Grubbles.'

The loudest cheer of the day erupted while Ticklechin slowly made his way to head of the table to sit down and listen to the song. He poked a finger in the jelly and had a little taste (which is really not very good manners, even for Boggles).

The Grubbles gathered into two groups as the villagers quietened down. Then, with a nod from Coney, they began. At first, the song was very quiet and peaceful with a lilting sound. The two groups sang different melodies, but they seemed to entwine with each other to create one beautiful rich refrain. They sang of the lovely Twiggle dancing they had seen and of the wonderful food before them. They sang of their adventures getting to Bewilderwood, and of their excitement at meeting Mildred.

As the song went on it became louder and at the same time more haunting. Everybody listening to it stood entranced. Even Ticklechin was like a statue, with one finger still in the jelly as though it was stuck. Finally the song ended, very quietly. There was a moment's silence then everybody clapped like mad. It was the most beautiful song they had ever heard.

Ticklechin rapped his stick on the ground again.

'Right, let the feast begin!' he declared.

But just as they were all about to tuck in to the mounds of food, they all heard Moss cry out.

'Help! Help everybody! It's Mildred. She's in the water and she doesn't look very well.'

Everyone rushed over to the edge of the platform and ran down to the jetty by the water. Mildred was there and she looked awful. Her eyelids were drooping and her smile seemed less than jolly. She was moaning a little. But the thing everybody noticed, most of all, was that she had turned a muddy colour of pink.

'I don't feel very good,' she announced. 'Not *th*pecially well, in fact.'

She coughed a horrible croaky cough, and wiped her forehead with the handkerchief Moss had given her.

All the villagers gathered round the jetty to help Mildred out of the water. She was groaning quite loudly and holding her tummy.

'We'd better get the Witch,' suggested Leaflette. 'She always knows the cure for things. I wonder where she is?'

'I'm just here,' said a voice behind them. The witch had already arrived, in that mysterious way she had of being in just the right place when she was needed.

'Let me have a look at the patient,' she suggested, and she took Mildred's pulse and put a gentle hand on her forehead.

Then she asked Mildred to stick out her tongue. It was a glowing colour of red.

'Mildred really is very sick, I'm afraid. She's got very bad grizzleberry poisoning. How on earth did she get that? Everyone knows not to eat grizzleberries'

Mildred explained about her bath and the nap by the fire and the spilt cauldron.

'I think the Grubbles might have something that could cure her,' suggested Swampy. 'They put it on the socks and it made them safe.'

'That's a very good suggestion,' said the witch, 'but it won't completely cure her I'm afraid, and there is one slight side effect. It will make her feel much better though.'

'Come on everybody,' cried Oakum. 'Get out your powder and sprinkle it on Mildred.'

All of the Grubbles dusted their powder onto Mildred and it fizzed as it found the grizzleberry stains. Mildred looked very relieved almost immediately, although she went even pinker than before.

'I'll give her a potion for her tummy too. It tastes nasty, but it should sort out Mildred's tummy ache,' said the witch. She produced a small phial and spooned a small amount of black syrup into Mildred's mouth.

'Not a*th* horrid a*th* pongiporridge,' pronounced Mildred, after making a few sour faces.

'Thank you very much. I feel a lot better now. Almost well enough for a bowl of that yummy clunknettle *th*oup I can *th*mell,' she declared.

A large bowl of soup was brought for her and she drank it

slowly, while a huge reed bed was made for her in the marshes. The witch told her to lie in the warm bed and not to exert herself too much, because the syrup hadn't fully cured her.

Mildred lay down and propped her head up on an elbow. She noticed that everybody was looking at her.

'Don't worry everyone. I feel fine now. You can go on with your party.'

'Actually we're a bit worried about the colour the powder has made you go,' whispered Swampy in Mildred's ear.

They brought Mildred a mirror and she looked at her face. It was now a very rich colour of pink. In fact, all of her was a very

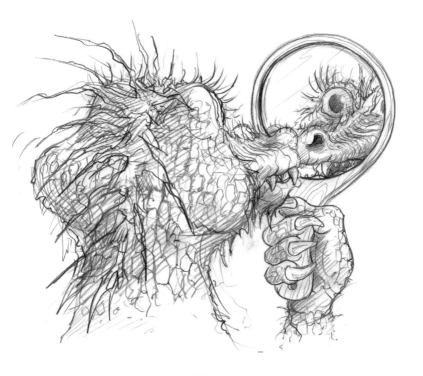

rich colour of pink. Just as the socks had got redder after being sprinkled, so had Mildred. It was the slight side-effect which the witch had mentioned. Mildred groaned when she saw what had happened.

'Although I like the colour very much, I don't think I want to *th*tay pink forever,' she announced.

'Even though you seem better, Mildred, you still aren't very well. You'll have to stay until we can get a cure and I'm afraid we don't have the ingredients in Bewilderwood,' explained the witch. 'The only place I know to get it is a long way from here where an old friend of mine lives. I'll set off in the morning and get it for you, but you'll be in bed for a couple of days. Meanwhile I'd better go with the Grubbles, to have a look at the Long Lagoon and see what trouble that grizzelberry juice has caused. I'm afraid we'd better delay the party until we have cleaned things up.'

As the witch and the Grubbles prepared to set off, Mildred beckoned to Swampy.'I'm *th*o *th*orry that I made *th*uch a lot of trouble. I know everything i*th* all my fault,' she whispered, miserably.

'It's not really your fault Mildred. You were fast asleep. I once sleepwalked out of my hut and fell into the marsh. That wasn't my fault either. It was just bad luck,' replied Swampy.

'Well, I'm *th*orry anyway,' said Mildred.

The
Long
Lagoon

When Grubbles want to move fast, they can be surprisingly zippy. The great flotilla of coracles sped down the Dismal Dyke, scattering flustered coots before them as they went. The witch was in Coney's boat, at the front. They were all very worried about what the grizzleberries might have done to the marsh.

As they came around the corner which led to the Long Lagoon, they saw what they had most feared. For near their campsite, where Mildred had tried to clean up the mess, there was no longer a tranquil scene of peaceful green reeds. The bulrushes were turning grey and wilting and all of the sedge and reeds drooped. Worse, there were a few coots and ducks swimming slowly about in circles looking very ill. The Grubbles paddled their coracles even faster and soon everyone had gathered around the terrible scene.

'We'd better sprinkle some dust on all these poor birds first, and then we'll see what we can do with the marsh,' the witch declared.

After a short while, there were a lot of much healthier-looking birds swimming around with pink feathers, chirruping and quacking gratefully.

'I think we've got a problem though,' Coney told the witch. 'The juice is everywhere and we haven't enough dust to clean it all up.'

The witch thought for a while. Eventually she said, 'I think we should save the last of that dust for any more sick birds and animals. There is only one person who can help us and I'm sure that she will be able clean everything up, but she lives a long way from here. She's a hippopotomuddle and she loves to clean mud. I was going to go to her myself, but with so many birds to look after, not to mention Mildred, I had better stay here, and I think the Grubbles had too. We'll all have our hands full trying to clean up. But we do need somebody to find her and bring her back.'

'I'll go, if you like,' offered Oakum. 'But I'd like Swampy to come with me, if he wants to. He is the best explorer in the village.'

'That is very brave of you, Oakum,' said the witch. 'Why not go back to the Boggle village and ask him. You might see if Willow would go along with you as well. There are some flowers you'll need to find, and she is the only person who knows which ones they are.'

So Oakum, Briar and Coney paddled their little boats back to the village, to see if their friends would join in the adventure.

When they arrived, they found Mildred sitting up in bed talking with the little Twiggle girls about handbags and bracelets. But she wasn't really her usual bouncy self and kept coughing from time to time.

There were a few difficulties gathering the party together as Willow had said that, although she did want to go, she wasn't

prepared to take Sticklenose on such a big journey. So Leaflette kindly offered to look after him while she was away. Willow spent a lot of time hugging and cuddling him before she handed him over to Leaflette.

'Be good my darling Sticklenose, and don't go climbing any trees while I'm away,' she said tearfully.

They went to join Swampy, who was asking Mildred if perhaps she wouldn't mind staying pink, and then perhaps they wouldn't have to go. But although Mildred said she could stay pink if she had to, it still didn't solve the problem of the polluted mud. So Swampy packed a bag full of lots of the delicious things that had been cooked for the huge feast and soon the three intrepid travellers were travelling by coracle to the Long Lagoon.

When they arrived, the witch gave them a map for the journey, saying, 'I'm afraid it is a long way and you'll have to camp for a night or two. But it really is the only way we can make things better.'

She gave Willow a small pouch containing a couple of potions and other useful things, and she described the orange flowers the hippopotomuddle would need for the cure.

'Those sound very like the flowers that we make our dust from,' said Oakum's dad.

Willow promised to gather a nice big bunch.

Oakum, Swampy and Willow said their goodbyes to the Grubbles before heading on their way. Oakum changed into Grubble clothes and was now wearing a blue and yellow robe his mother had made. He borrowed one of the Grubble coracles. He folded it up carefully and strapped it to his back.

All three of them took big sacks of food, which they tied onto poles and carried over their shoulders.

Just as they were leaving, Coney came over with a large green bowl of pongiporridge, with the strange vapour still drifting lazily over the edge.

'You shouldn't go travelling if you are hungry, so I thought you might like a bite before you leave.'

But the three of them all agreed that it was more important to get on and find the hippopotomuddle as soon as possible.

The
Mellow
Meadows

The Long Lagoon was a good place to set off on their journey as it was right on the edge of Bewilderwood. The far shore was studded with hundreds of small bushes, which bore exquisite little yellow fruit in autumn, but were now covered in tiny white blooms. Between the bushes was grass, studded with daisies. Willow thought the whole place was lovely and if they hadn't been so worried about Mildred and the mud, they might have stopped to enjoy the flowers.

It was very easy travelling though. Willow checked the map and used her compass from time to time. The compass was one of the things the witch had given her, and it was magical. It was made of a clear bluish crystal and when you looked through it, a little glint of light pointed out the right way.

After a while the bushes thinned out and, eventually, there was only a lovely meadow that seemed to stretch on and on forever.

'Although I've never been this far from home before, it's hard to be frightened in such a beautiful place,' said Willow. She leaned down and picked a few tiny purple flowers, which she made into a chain to wear in her hair.

Oakum sang some Twiggle songs as he marched along and everyone felt merrier. Even Swampy said he didn't mind

46

adventures when the going was as easy as this. All the same, he thought, it might help to have a little snack.

'Not yet, Swampy,' argued Willow. 'We'll have to be careful with the food on this trip or we might run out later. The sun will set in a while. When it does, we'll make a camp and we can eat then.'

Swampy looked wistfully at his bundle. He could almost hear the welcoming sound of his first bite of nutbug crunch. But he agreed that Willow was right.

As the sun began to slowly set among the tiny pink wisps of cloud, the whole great meadow was lit with a soft golden light. There seemed to be a gentle magic in the air.

The wide meadow began to have less grass and there were

more sandy areas. Soon, they were walking through little tussocks dotted amongst soft sand. The sun was low in the sky now and there was an orange pink hue to the light.

'I think we should make our camp soon,' said Oakum.

'I'll get the food out then,' offered Swampy.

While Swampy laid out a sweetsludge pie and barkicrisps on a blanket, Oakum put up the tent he was carrying. It threw a very long, pointed shadow.

Willow made a fire from the little bits of brushwood they had gathered and soon the three travellers were enjoying a tasty meal. It was much better than usual because the Boggles put extra-special treats in the sweetsludge pie for really big feasts. This one was particularly good.

'I do wish little Sticklenose was here too. I miss him,' sighed Willow.

Swampy put an arm around Willow's shoulders and said, 'I'm sure he'll be fine with Leaflette. She's really good with babies.'

Oakum finished his pie, lay back with a bundle for a pillow and began cleaning his teeth with a twig. Suddenly he sat up, pointing. 'What's that in the sky over there,' he exclaimed.

Far away, in the distance, was what looked like an enormous black bird with very long legs. Swampy felt a shiver run down his back. He wondered why travelling always seemed to involve meeting enormous beasts who might eat you up. But as the bird came closer, they could see that it was actually two bats carrying something. Or, as it turned out, someone. With a flurry of black wings, Snagglefang and Beaker landed at the camp. What they were carrying was little Sticklenose.

'We found him on the Twiggle village platform. We thought

you'd forgotten the little fellow,' explained Snagglefang.

Willow was hugging Sticklenose and making cooing noises. Then she turned to the bats. 'But he was supposed to be there. Poor Leaflette must be frantic with worry,' she fretted.

The bats looked crestfallen.

'We're so sorry. We didn't think of that. We just thought you would be pleased,' said Beaker. 'I'll fly back straight away and tell her where he is.'

And in a second, he was off. All they could see of him was a tiny black dot disappearing into the orange sky.

'It's lovely to see you dear Sticklenose. But I'll just give you a goodnight kiss and Snagglefang will take you back home.' Willow said, hugging the baby Twiggle.

49

Snagglefang coughed a little.

'I can't do that, I'm afraid. I needed Beaker's help to bring him hear. I'm not strong enough on my own.'

Snagglefang looked so forlorn at having done the wrong thing that even Willow couldn't be angry with him.

'Well, I'm sure he'll be safe enough with us. Even though he is very young to go on an adventure,' she decided.

Sticklenose looked delighted.

'Would you like some nutbug crunch before you go?' asked Oakum, offering Snagglefang a bagful.

'Thank you, I would,' said Snagglefang, enthusiastically. 'But I thought I might stay if you don't mind. I met the witch and she told me where you were. She thought it might be a good idea if I came along, as it could be useful having someone about who can fly.'

'Of course you are welcome to join us. It's always nice to have someone with fierce teeth with you on a journey,' said Swampy, adding, 'I mean, only if they are on your side.'

'I am most definitely on your side,' smiled Snagglefang.

'Well, it will be a long day tomorrow so we'd better settle down to sleep,' Willow suggested.

They all snuggled up inside Oakum's tent for the night, which was rather a tight squeeze. It helped that Snagglefang slept upside down at the top.

'Nighty night,' whispered Sticklenose to his mother, and then they were all asleep.

It wasn't an easy night though because, it turned out, Snagglefang snored very loudly.

The DRY Desert

When they woke up, the sun was already blazing in the bright blue sky.

'It'll be a hot day today,' observed Swampy to nobody in particular, as he laid out food for breakfast.

It had been quite dark when they made camp the night before and they hadn't been able to really see what sort of place they were in. In fact, they had travelled as far as the grasslands went. In front of them, stretching as far as the eye could see, was a great rolling sandy desert. Nothing grew there.

'The compass says we need to cross that desert,' said Willow. 'I'm glad Sticklenose was wearing his hat last night. It should protect him from the sun.'

Snagglefang looked very pleased. The hat had been a present from him, and all the other bats. Sticklenose almost never took it off.

'Maybe Snagglefang should fly ahead and see what is the best way to go,' suggested Swampy.

'I don't think I'll try flying just yet. It always takes me a little while to find my morning wings,' replied Snagglefang. He rubbed his tummy a little carefully.

After breakfast, they tied the tent to Oakum's back and set off. At first, it was a very nice walk. The ground was firm and the sun was warm. Soon they left the grasslands behind and all around them was dry sandy desert. There was one absolutely tiny cloud in the sky. In front of them, the horizon shimmered. As they carried on it became hotter and hotter.

After a while Oakum wiped his brow. 'We'll need to find water soon. I don't think that we have brought quite enough,' he said.

'Here's a clever thing which the witch gave me,' said Willow, producing what looked like a bit of green rope. 'You hold it at this end and twirl it round and when it stops spinning, it always points to water.'

She twirled it above her head and then stopped. The rope wriggled for a bit and then pointed straight at Swampy.

'I think it's only found my water bottle,' he said. 'Maybe there isn't any water here at all.'

They agreed that the best thing to do was to keep going, but to be very careful about rationing the water. They gave more to Sticklenose though, because babies need lots of water.

After consulting the compass, they trudged wearily forwards. The sand was deeper here and sometimes each step was difficult. Snagglefang gave up walking and flew ahead, stopping to wait for the others to catch up. Each time they did, he had the same thing to say to them. 'I'm afraid there's nothing but more desert, as far as the eye can see,' he reported gloomily.

So they kept on travelling through the light desert sand with the great yellow sun beating down from a perfect blue sky.

Behind them, their footsteps led back in a long thin line to the dry horizon.

'Why don't we tell riddles to pass the time,' suggested Snagglefang.

Without waiting for a reply he asked, 'Why can you never starve in the desert?' But before anyone could say anything, he burst out with the answer: 'Because of all the sandwiches there. Get it? Sand-which-is-there. Sandwiches.'

Nobody laughed much.

'That's one of my better jokes,' complained Snagglefang.

'It's quite a good joke, but we've all heard it before,' explained Swampy.

Suddenly Sticklenose burst out in giggles.

'Sticklenose likes sandwiches. Good jokey, Snagglefang,' he chortled.

Snagglefang looked happier. 'Here's another one. Why is the desert such a spooky place?' he asked.

None of them knew the answer.

'Because of all the sand-witches there. You know – witches . . . with broomsticks.'

Nobody laughed at all.

'Isn't that the same joke again?' asked Oakum.

'And the witch isn't spooky,' protested Swampy.

'I really miss my gang of Bewilderbats,' muttered Snagglefang. He went quite quiet after that.

Eventually, Sticklenose demanded his lunch.

Swampy was just laying out the blanket for the picnic and putting out the food when he suddenly exclaimed, 'There's no nutbug crunch. We must have left it behind.'

'No, I'm certain we didn't leave anything behind at the camp. I checked,' said Willow.

Swampy noticed that Snagglefang was creeping away from the others.

'Did you eat the nutbug crunch, Snagglefang?' he accused.

'I got a little peckish in the night,' confessed Snagglefang. 'But I didn't eat it all.'

'Where is it then?' demanded Swampy.

'I gave the rest to Sticklenose. He likes his nutbug crunch, I must say.'

Willow was quite cross and made Snagglefang promise not to take any more food.

They had a nice lunch though, as there were plenty of seedi-buns and, of course, the excellent sweetsludge pie.

They set off again straight after they had eaten, despite Swampy's protestations that a little lie-down was always a good idea after any meal.

There was no change in the landscape though. Sand, more sand, and, after that, some more sand.

Oakum sang a few songs to cheer them up, and they all enjoyed his singing.

After an hour or so of walking, Swampy noticed that Snagglefang was missing. He pointed this out to the others.

'Something is coming towards us over the top of that dune just there?' Oakum pointed out.

It was Snagglefang, with something very large in his mouth. It looked like an old hessian sack full of something. He was flying very slowly and nearly crashing into the top of the sand dunes, as he struggled with the weight. They watched as he weaved his way towards them. When he arrived, he dropped his bundle and lay on the sand gasping for breath. They gave him some water and he began to sit up.

'I've got some more food for us. I didn't realise that the supplies were running out when I ate the nutbug crunch, so I went and found some more.'

'But where did you get it out here?' asked Swampy.

'I met a tribesman out in the desert, riding a very funny looking horse. I flew over and asked him if he could spare some food. He gave me this,' replied Snagglefang.

He opened the sack and out poured hundreds of dates.

'They're delicious,' said Snagglefang. 'Try one.'

They all ate some dates and decided that they were easily as good as nutbug crunch.

'Although it's quite difficult swallowing the hard bit in the middle,' complained Oakum.

They explained that you were supposed to spit that bit out.

'That was very nice of the tribesman to give us his food. I hope he won't be hungry,' said Swampy.

'Well, he didn't exactly give me them. I had to buy them,' explained Snagglefang.

'What with?' enquired Willow.

'Oh, I found a sort of pretty rock, so I gave him that,' said Snagglefang.

Willow searched in her bag and then stared at Snagglefang.

'You couldn't have given away our compass, Snagglefang?' Willow cried.

'Is that what it was?' said Snagglefang. 'I thought it was just a nice rock.'

'Oh Snagglefang!' said Willow in a sad voice.

'We've still got the map,' Oakum pointed out. 'We'll have to make do with that.'

They pulled out the map and, after making Snagglefang promise not to sell that too, they tried to work out where they were. It seemed that they needed to find a river, which would lead them to the place where the hippopotomuddle lived, all the way on the other side of the desert.

Then they ate more dates, which were sweet and juicy and very, very good.

The Delicious Dates

In really dry deserts, it can be quite hard work walking. As they clambered to the top of the great dunes the travellers slid back down the sand almost as far as they had climbed. On the other hand, sliding down the other side of the dunes was great fun. Oakum, with his big round tummy, found that rolling over and over was the fastest way to get to the bottom. Swampy and the others, slid down. But, each time they had enjoyed a lovely dusty dune slide, there was another high slope of sand to climb up. It was thirsty work. They all tried to ration their water, but soon there wasn't much left.

'I think we should have another try with the water rope,' suggested Willow.

So she twirled it round her head again and when it stopped, it wriggled a little and then pointed at Swampy again.

'But I've drunk all my water,' Swampy protested.

'I'm afraid it thinks you are water, Swampy,' said Snaggle-fang sadly.

'How unusual of the witch to give us something that doesn't work,' said Willow.

'Maybe it does work, though,' Oakum said thoughtfully.

'Perhaps it wasn't pointing at Swampy. Maybe it was pointing *through* Swampy.'

So Swampy moved and Willow did another twirl of the rope. This time it pointed at where Swampy used to be.

'You're right Oakum. How clever you are. It does know where water is. I'm sure we'll be alright now!' cried Swampy, clapping his friend on the back. Oakum looked very pleased to have been some help. Swampy was also quite relieved that the water rope didn't really think he was water. He was almost sure you couldn't drink Boggles, but still, it was better if nobody ever tried to.

So the travellers followed the rope's directions. It was becoming another really hot day and there still was nothing but yellow sand wherever they looked, but everybody felt more hopeful.

Then, as they reached the very top of an extra big sand dune, they finally saw what they had been searching for. Far down, below them, was a great green oasis with a lake and beyond the lake stretched out the most beautiful valley, filled with green palm trees and pretty cactus plants. Even better, there was a long blue river winding sleepily through the middle of the valley.

Everybody ran down the dune as fast as they could in a flurry of arms and legs. Oakum was caught up in Snagglefang's wings for a little while, but in a very few moments everyone was at the lake's edge, drinking the clean flowing water. Then they all jumped in, and they were soon jumping about and playing happily.

Sticklenose was sitting contentedly in the sandy shallows,

splashing with both arms and blowing bubbles in the clear water.

'Lovely splashybubbles,' he announced.

Soon they were all blowing bubbles in the water too.

Willow consulted her map.

'We need to follow this river out of the desert,' she announced.

'If we use my coracle, the current of the river will make us go quicker,' suggested Oakum. 'But it will be a bit of a tight squeeze.'

They assembled the small boat and, somehow, everyone managed to climb in. Snagglefang decided that boats were not for him, so he flew just above the others. They hardly had to paddle as the river was flowing quite quickly and soon they were making good progress.

There was a little bit of trouble when Swampy tried to organise a small snack.

'The boat is so full, I can't reach the sweetsludge pie,' he complained.

'Don't wriggle like that or we'll capsize,' warned Oakum, but it was too late. With a tipping lurch, everybody was splashing about in the water and the boat was upside down. Swampy was diving down deep into the river to retrieve his bag of food. Little Sticklenose was happily perched on Willow's back as she swam towards the shore.

'More splashies,' he observed cheerfully.

Swampy eventually made it to shore, where he found Oakum repairing his little craft.

'I'm very sorry but I've lost the food,' Swampy stated mournfully. 'And I've made everybody wet too.'

'You shouldn't wriggle about in a little boat,' said Oakum.

Swampy looked miserable.

Willow put an arm around his shoulder and said, 'It's alright. I've still got a little food in my bag and we've got the dates too. Also, it's lovely and warm so we'll dry out in no time.'

'I don't think we do have the dates anymore,' said Snaggle-fang sadly. 'I think they fell out of the boat too.'

The travellers looked very worried at this. Supper tonight was going to be a rather hungry one and after that, what would they do? They decided not to eat anything until then.

They climbed back into the boat and paddled along the river. Everyone seemed to be much quieter now, except for some rumbling noises made by Swampy's tummy.

Snagglefang announced that all this flying was making him tired and he needed a rest. There wasn't really enough room in the boat for him to put his feet up there, so he announced that he would pop over to the palm trees and have a nap.

'I'll catch you up in a while,' he said, as he flapped across to a tall palm tree and settled in, upside down, to rest. Suddenly he began shouting and flapping. He seemed to be pulling at something and, to the travellers in the boat, it looked like he was having a fight. They were just paddling over to him as fast as they could, to see if they could help, when Snagglefang fell out of the tree wrestling with what looked like a great big bobbly creature. He managed to regain his wings just before he hit the ground and then he flew slowly towards the other travellers.

'I've found something! I've saved us!' he was shouting.

As he flew towards the coracle, the travellers could see that he hadn't been fighting with a creature at all. He had been pulling a huge bunch of juicy dates free of the tree. There was more than enough to eat now.

'Well done Snagglefang! You're brilliant,' shouted Swampy, relieved.

Willow was muttering something about selling the compass, what with dates turning out to be free, but everybody was so relieved to find food that they didn't listen to her.

Then Oakum pointed forwards with excitement.

'That's the end of the river. We're nearly there,' he cried.

The river was widening into a great delta and beyond that, across a great sea of perfect water lilies, they could just make out the edge of a jungle. Fluttering over the great white water lily flowers were hundreds of shiny blue dragonflies, skipping this way and that. After all the dry sand of the desert, it seemed to Swampy to be a calm and perfect sight.

'Let's camp on the bank and cross that tomorrow,' suggested Willow and, as soon as Swampy had swallowed his date, he agreed with her. So they dragged the little boat out of the water and found a small patch of soft grass under some palm trees to put up the tent. They didn't really need to because, after they had eaten and made a nice fire, they found it was warm enough to sleep outside.

They lay on their backs around the fire, tucked snugly under their blankets. Oakum and Swampy were quietly picking their teeth with small twigs.

'Don't the stars look even brighter and shinier out here,' Oakum remarked.

Above them, they gazed at a huge purple sky, twinkling with soft silver stars.

'Isn't it pretty, Sticklenose, my darling,' murmered Willow gently.

But Sticklenose replied with tiny happy snores.

Meeting Minty

Dawn on the edge of a jungle is a lovely time of day, especially when you have been sleeping outside. Pink wisps of clouds were drifting through deep turquoise skies. The white water-lily flowers were glowing in the soft yellow light of the rising sun and the dragonflies were just waking up, gently stretching their flickering blue wings on the huge green lily pads.

Swampy was the first to open his eyes. As he admired the beautiful day, he made himself useful by laying out the breakfast. There was only the small bit of sweetsludge pie that Willow had saved, some barkicrisps and the enormous pile of dates. He took a few of the dates over to the water's edge, sat down on the bank and began to eat them lazily, as he watched the sun rise in the sky. The scene seemed so peaceful that he began to wonder what life would be like if he wasn't a Marsh Boggle after all, but instead, lived here all the time. But then he thought to himself: 'I bet that it's not always as perfect as this. Maybe something is lurking out there that might want to eat me up.' And after that he decided, although this place was lovely, it would still be nice to go home in the end.

The rest of the travellers were soon awake, yawning and stretching their arms. They were pleased to see the breakfast laid out for them.

'I do like dates,' said Oakum, 'although it might be nice to find something else to eat as well. They are very sweet.'

'That's what is best about them,' protested Snagglefang.

Sticklenose helped himself to more dates, adding: 'Yummy food.'

'All the same, I wouldn't mind a bowl of pongiporridge just now,' declared Oakum.

'*Yeuch!*' muttered Swampy. But he agreed, it was nice if there was a change of diet from time to time.

Soon the boat was assembled and they were on their way across the great lake of water-lilies, with Snagglefang flying just above them. They paddled carefully between the leaves and flowers and, in a while, the shore was a long way behind them.

'Did anyone else see those lily pads moving over there,' Willow asked nervously.

But nobody had.

'I hope there aren't any scary creatures living in the water,' said Swampy. 'We've come too far to be eaten up now.'

'I'm sure nothing will eat us, Swampy,' said Willow, but she didn't sound certain. Then she pointed. 'There it is again.'

Something was making the lily pads bob about in the water. Whatever it was, it was under the surface. It was quite a long way away and it was moving in a zig-zag pattern.

'It probably hasn't seen us,' suggested Oakum. 'Let's keep very still and hope that it goes away.'

But instead, it was getting much closer to the boat. As it approached, the five travellers could see that it was moving quite fast and in an apparently random pattern. Suddenly

Oakum shouted: 'Paddle! Quick! It's coming straight for us.'

Swampy grabbed the paddle and tried to move the small boat away, but it was too late. With a great big bump, there was a huge crash and everybody was splashing about in the water. The coracle was upside down once again.

'Gosh! Bother! What happened?' demanded a loud squeaky voice, which didn't sound like any of the travellers.

Everybody was now splashing their way back to the boat and holding on to its side, except for Snagglefang, who was sitting, quite dry, on top of the hull. Sticklenose clambered onto Willow's shoulders.

'More splashies!' he said contentedly, hugging his mother's head.

They looked around for the creature who had turned their little craft over. It wasn't long before a tiny green head, with smiling jaws, bobbed up out of the water. It looked like a much smaller and very green version of Mildred, with huge dark shiny eyes.

'Hello!' it said. 'I'm Minty. I'm called Minty because I'm green. I'm a crocklebog. What on earth are you doing swimming about here?'

'We weren't swimming until you hit our boat,' complained Oakum, as he splashed towards his little craft.

'So that's what happened. Golly. It's a terrible nuisance too, because I was just about to beat my record for underwater swimming,' announced Minty brightly.

'You might have looked where you were going,' Willow suggested.

'My mummy always says that too. It's just that I'm still a

very small crocklebog and I haven't got the hang of opening my eyes underwater yet. In fact, I'm only allowed to practice out here in the lake because at home I bump into everything. Other than you, there aren't any accidents to have out here,' explained Minty, before asking: 'Do you have anything to eat. Trying for records makes me quite hungry.'

She seemed so friendly that there was no point in being cross, and after all, nobody had been hurt. Also, because of Swampy's earlier accident, they had tied the remaining food to the bottom of the boat and when they turned it back over, the right way up, it was still there. Sticklenose and Willow clambered in with help from the others, but Oakum and Swampy weren't quite the right shape for getting over the side easily, so they just held on to the edge and swam in the water. Willow gave Minty some dates.

She chewed them carefully and announced that she wasn't sure about the squishy bit on the outside, but that the pips in the middle were scrummy.

'Why don't you come to my home to get dry? Mummy will be so pleased to meet you,' she suggested. She seemed such a friendly sort of crocklebog, they all agreed immediately.

But with Oakum and Swampy hanging on to the boat in the water, they were going very slowly. Snagglefang suggested that if Minty held a rope in her teeth, with the other end tied to the boat, they would go much faster.

'What about this bit of string?' asked Minty, holding up the magical water rope that the witch had given them. She twirled it about gaily in her mouth. Immediately the stick on the end of the string began to quiver as it looked for water. First it whirled round and round in a circle around Minty's head, and then the string shot straight up in the air and knotted itself into a spiral.

Minty handed it back to Willow.

'Not very well behaved, that bit of rope. Perhaps we could use another one,' she requested.

'I don't think anyone has asked it to find water in the middle of a lake before. It must have upset it,' she explained to Minty.

The magic string was put down on the seat of the boat, where it lay twitching every now and then, as Willow stroked it gently. It seemed to be calming down.

Eventually they found a different piece of rope. It had been helping to hold up Oakum's trousers, but luckily he was wearing braces too, so he didn't mind lending it. Snagglefang's idea worked really well and they were pulled by the little crocklebog, at a surprisingly fast pace, through the lily leaves to the other side of the lake.

Snagglefang sat in the boat this time, holding onto Sticklenose, who thought that this was an excellent way to travel. He was leaning over the side to let his hand trail in the rushing water. This was quite safe except that, every now and then, Sticklenose tried to grab a passing water-lily flower, and once he nearly fell out. So Willow held him after that.

When they reached the edge, they found a bank, to pull up to, among the tangled dark green bushes. Swampy and Oakum, who were really very soaked by now, clambered back into the boat gratefully.

Swampy noticed that all the trees were bursting with plump purple fruit.

'Can you eat these?' he asked Minty.

'Yes you can. They're junglifigs. But they are very squishy and I don't much like them,' she replied.

Swampy tried one, and it was sweet and creamy. Soon everyone had eaten a few, and some more were placed carefully in the bottom of the boat for later.

Just as they were about to leave, Willow spotted some little orange flowers.

'I'm sure those are the flowers that the witch asked me to pick. She said that they would grow very near the lake,' said Willow.

The delicate flowers were rather small and not many people would have noticed them. Swampy congratulated Willow on spotting them. They picked a large bunch and then they climbed back into the boat.

Everybody followed Minty along the edge of the lake for a while. Snagglefang rode on Minty's back, as the overhanging trees made flying quite tricky. Then, Minty darted through a small river opening which led straight back into the jungle.

At first the water followed a mazy route through fig trees and mangroves, but slowly the water became browner and the scenery began to change. They were slowly entering the hugest, greenest place any of them had ever seen. Everywhere were trees so tall that they couldn't really see the sky, and long vines dangled, like rigging, from their branches. Along the river banks were enormous fronds of emerald leaves bursting upwards from the ground. Each one was taller than Swampy. There were giant yellow butterflies, while little creatures scampered above them in the high canopy. It felt like a happy place with all the insects and creatures bustling all about them, making plenty of loud chatter.

'Nearly there now,' exclaimed Minty, enthusiastically, and she disappeared under the water as she swam round in excited circles. Snagglefang was still sitting on her and only just managed to fly off her back in the nick of time. The little crockle-bog surfaced again and pointed to a small opening in the side of the riverbank, which was overhung with climbing roses.

'Our front door,' she explained. 'Daddy's away exploring, but you can come in and meet my mummy.'

She shot into the house.

As Oakum steered his boat through the entrance carefully, they could hear Minty up ahead, shouting 'Yoo hoo! Mummy! I'm home . . . '

Inside the rose-covered doorway was a brownish pond with

bushes growing all around it. Draped on many of the bushes were lots of brightly coloured scarves and each bush was laden with a different type of fruit. Swampy thought to himself having your own food growing inside your own house was a very, very clever idea indeed.

Minty emerged from under an especially thick bush, grinning cheerily.

'Mummy's home and she's just coming,' she announced.

The Humid House

On the far side of the small brown pond there was a nice dry place to climb out of the boat. Willow climbed out first and was trying to make Sticklenose a little more presentable, while he wriggled in her arms. Poor old Swampy and Oakum looked a very bedraggled pair, after all that swimming with their clothes on. They were rather embarrassed at meeting someone new in such a state. Then the bushes began rustling and out of the thick leaves emerged a large thorny crocklebog. She looked very like Mildred, except that she was dressed in a mauve headscarf and was wearing lots of brightly coloured bracelets.

'Hello everyone. My daughter has told me all about you. I'm so happy to have you to stay. My name is Millicent,' the creature announced.

Everyone all said hello to Millicent.

'Please help yourselves to my berry bushes. Those pink ones with the white spots over there are very good. Then let's have a cosy chat,' Millicent said. She had one of those soft gentle voices which made her sound as if she was in a dream. Everybody had a few berries, and Snagglefang gave Millicent some dates.

'I've not tried these before. They have delicious pips,' she said.

'We don't eat those. We call them stones, and they give us tummy ache,' explained Oakum.

'Perhaps you didn't crunch them up enough. Ah, here is my daughter. I called her Minty because she is green. I think people should look like their names,' she explained.

'But aren't all crocklebogs green?' asked Swampy.

'Well, Minty and me are certainly green. I'm not sure if all the others are the same colour though,' replied Milicent. 'But where have you met any crocklebogs? We mostly live here in the jungle, and you're all new here.'

'Actually, it's because of another crocklebog that we came, only she's pink and we're trying to help her,' explained Willow.

'But I thought you said all crocklebogs were green,' said a confused-looking Millicent.

So they explained that the crocklebog they were talking about was once green, but that the juice the Grubbles had given her had turned her pink. Then they told her of all the adventures they had crossing the desert and the lake.

'We are looking for the hippopotomuddle. Do you know her?' asked Oakum.

'Of course I know her. She's a tremendous friend,' said Millicent. 'I was only saying the other day to Minty that we should invite her to drop by for a nice cup of mudslush tea.'

'Do you think we could we meet her?' asked Swampy.

'Of course you could. We could go and find her right away if you like,' said Millicent. 'Only give me a minute to pick out the right scarf. I do like to be dressed properly when I make visits.'

She perused the bushes, picking up different scarves and trying them on, only to reject each one and then trying another.

'Mildred will be so pleased,' remarked Swampy to Willow. 'I bet she's had enough of being pink by now.'

'Did you say Mildred?' Millicent asked Swampy. 'Only I have a sister called Mildred, but she moved away a long time ago. She used to have lots of handbags and jewellery.'

'That's our friend, Mildred!' shouted all the travellers at once.

'Goodness me! Well, I'm glad to know where she is but I don't like the sound of her being ill. Minty and I had better join you on your journey, and go and visit her. I'll have to pack even more clothes now.'

Millicent began picking large piles of headscarves, shaking her head at them thoughtfully and then putting them back on to the bushes very carefully.

'Why don't you take all of your scarves. There's plenty of room in my bag,' suggested Willow.

Millicent decided that this was a very good idea.

They were almost ready to leave when Willow suddenly asked: 'Where on earth has Sticklenose got to?'

'Minty and Snagglefang aren't here either,' said Oakum.

Just then, they heard a noisy commotion outside the rose-covered doorway. They ran to see what was happening. On the other side of the river they could see Sticklenose, riding on Minty's back. They were racing after Snagglefang as he flew along the muddy water.

'Don't do any diving Minty dear,' Millicent called across the water, before turning to Willow and saying in her dreamy voice: 'She's a tremendous diver you know. Terribly good at it.'

Willow was shouting: 'Hold on tight Sticklenose! Come on back! Don't dive Minty!'

But Minty didn't dive.

Shortly, everyone was ready to go.

The Hippopotamuddle

There was quite a lot to carry, because, it turned out crockle-bogs are not very quick at packing. In truth, it seemed that there wasn't anything that they didn't put in their bags, except for the bracelets. Millicent just wore all of those instead. Also, Minty kept trying on her things before putting them in her suitcase to show the others how nice they were. But eventually, they were off.

Minty led the way, wearing a pair of pink fluffy wings which hadn't fitted easily into the bags and which she had insisted on taking along.

'Follow me everyone. I know the way off by heart,' said Minty, jumping up and down with the excitement of the adventure.

She led them to the back of the crocklebog's pool, and into the very thick jungle. Fortunately, there were paths through the great thickets of dark-leafed bushes. Above were the enormous branches of the huge trees with vines and creepers dangling down. Very little light could get through all of the leaves. All around were deafening noises from all the insects and animals in the bushes and trees, but the leaves were so dense that the travellers couldn't ever quite see what it was that was making such a tremendous din. Altogether, it was quite a scary sort of place.

Swampy felt, although there might be lots of fierce creatures about who might want a Boggle-sized snack, it was difficult to be too frightened, when you could see a little green crocklebog wearing pink clip-on wings zooming up and down the paths ahead, urging everyone to hurry up.

If they could, they would have gone faster, except that Millicent was quite slow. She insisted on stopping from time to time to adjust her rather fetching blue lace headscarf until it was on just right.

'It's important to look your best when you are visiting some-one,' she explained.

They did have to rescue Minty, when she caught her wings in one of the bushes, but otherwise the journey went well. The paths soon became straighter and suddenly they emerged from the dark gloom of the jungle into a great clearing. The blazing sunlight seemed to be twice as bright as usual after the murky bushes. Everyone rubbed their eyes as they adjusted to the sudden change.

They were in a huge grassy clearing, surrounded on all sides by the emerald jungle. In the middle was a great muddy lake. Dotted around it were piles of gooey mud, steaming slightly in the balmy air. There was a comfortable marshy smell to the place.

'I'll go and find the hippopotamuddle, shall I?' suggested Minty enthusiastically, and before anyone answered, she was off bouncing through the mud with her pink wings flapping on her back, shouting: 'Yoo Hoo! Hello! Are you there? It's me.'

She disappeared into the jungle on the other side of the clearing.

While they waited, Oakum and Swampy laid out some food for the hippopotamuddle. There was a small amount of sweetsludge pie left in Willow's food bag and a few barkicrisps. She hoped the hippopotamuddle would like them.

Snagglefang took Sticklenose off to tell him some more of his jokes, while Millicent found a grassy mound nearby and stretched out on top of it. She had a quick rummage through her headscarf collection, making sure she was wearing the right one but finally decided that she was. Then she busied herself rearranging her bangles. Eventually, she concluded that she was properly dressed so she lay down on her side, propping up her smiling head on one paw, ready to greet the hippopotamuddle.

'One must make a good impression on people,' she explained to Willow.

Then, in the far distance, they saw a pair of pink fluffy wings bouncing out of the jungle, followed by a huge grey creature walking after Minty in a slow gentle waddle. As she approached, they could see that it was the hippopotamuddle. She was wearing a white cotton bonnet and a big white frilly apron. Both were hand-embroidered with tiny little blue flowers. She looked a very friendly sort of creature.

After everybody had said hello and introduced themselves, the hippopotamuddle sat down to eat. She took a little time learning everybody's name and told the travellers that her own name was Vera.

'I've saved you some sweetsludge pie, Vera,' said Willow.

But when she looked for it she found that there wasn't any sweetsludge pie anymore.

Willow turned immediately to find Snagglefang, in case he had stolen it, but both he and Sticklenose were still by the edge of the jungle, laughing together at each other's riddles.

'It wasn't me,' protested Swampy before Willow could question him.

'I'm afraid, my dears, I may have just found your pie,' said the hippopotamuddle, apologetically. 'I think I might have sat on it.' She stood up slowly. Underneath her was a very flat, sticky mess. Even Swampy didn't think he could eat it now.

Oakum tried to help her clean it up, but the big hippopotamuddle didn't really need any help. From a pouch in her pinafore she produced some sponges and soap and, in a few seconds, the mess was gone.

'Cleaning is what I do best,' she explained. 'But I can be a bit clumsy I'm afraid. Now, Minty tells me you want to turn her pink and you need my help. I don't know what I can do, but I'm not sure if I don't prefer her green.'

It took a while, but eventually everybody managed to explain the real situation with Mildred and the problem with the marshes being poisoned by grizzleberries.

'And we don't want to turn Minty pink, either,' said Willow firmly.

Minty looked very disappointed.

'I must say that grizzleberries are extremely dangerous things so I don't think we should use them on Minty. But I would be very pleased to help you all. What I like to do best is cleaning up mud, and the mud here is in terribly good condition now.

I could do with a new challenge. I've got everything I need to fix your problem, except for turning Mildred back to her normal colour. To do that, I shall need to bring some special flowers and I haven't any.'

'The witch said these might be the ones you need,' suggested Willow, holding out the little orange flowers she had picked earlier.

'How clever you are. Those pretty flowers are the very ones I want,' said the hippopotamuddle. 'Excellent. Well then, we should be off soon, if we want to get there by tonight.'

'But it took us ages to get here,' said Swampy. 'How can we get back so quickly?'

'There is another way to Bewilderwood,' the hippopotamuddle explained. 'We can go by the Rapid River. My cousin has a boat and I'm sure he'll have us there in no time.'

So everybody packed their things up, while Millicent changed her scarf for another which was more suitable for boating. She chose a shiny yellow one with black sequins.

Snagglefang and Sticklenose had been playing hide-and-seek and it took some time to find Snagglefang, because he thought everybody was just joining in the game.

Then they followed the big grey hippopotamuddle as she waddled and swayed her way towards the Rapid River.

The Rapid River

The Rapid River wasn't far away. When they found it, it didn't seem very rapid. It was a wide, tranquil, greenish river with lots of overhanging trees and fronds. As they looked about they could see a rather dilapidated jetty made of grey poles. Tied to the jetty was a boat with a big black funnel in the middle. It was the biggest boat Swampy had ever seen. But what really took the eye was that it was painted a brilliant shade of purple. Lounging at the stern was something that looked like another very large hippopotamuddle, with a black pork pie hat pulled over his eyes. He was making gentle snoring noises.

'What a nice cheerful colour for a boat. We ought to paint ours like that too,' Oakum remarked.

'I thought all boats were purple,' said the hippopotamuddle. 'It seems to be the best colour for them. Although I suppose pink could be pretty too.'

'I like bright green,' said Minty, firmly. 'But purple is nice as well. Can we get in now?'

'I'll just go on board and wake the skipper first,' the hippopotamuddle said. 'He's another hippopotamuddle, but everyone in the jungle just calls him Captain.'

With a very stately waddle, she ambled over the jetty towards

the boat. There were several alarming-sounding groaning noises from the ancient jetty boards, but nothing broke. She poked the sleeping hippopotamuddle gently with her foot.

Nothing happened.

Vera nudged him a bit harder and he stirred a little, but then he resumed his snoring.

Meanwhile, Minty had rushed on to the boat and was beginning to explore it.

'Whoa! Golly! This is a big boat. I bet it has gone to loads of great places,' she said, enthusiastically. She started to examine all of the little holes and crannies on the purple craft. Before long, she had managed to get her head stuck in one of the holes. She wriggled and pushed with all four feet against the steep side of the boat in her efforts to get free. Suddenly, with a pop, she shot out backwards and bounced straight towards the sleeping captain. She hit him squarely on the nose.

The captain woke up with a start, rubbing his snout.

'Whatever is that,' he said, sounding very alarmed.

'Hello!' said Minty brightly. 'I'm Minty. I've come to have a go on your boat.'

The hippopotamuddle rubbed his eyes in surprise, while he adjusted his cap. He had never seen a crocklebog with pink wings before. But he was an experienced traveller, and had seen all kinds of strange things before. He decided that Minty probably wasn't too dangerous a creature. Then he saw Vera, so he smiled a happy hello to her.

Vera explained to him that they all wanted to take the boat to Bewilderwood so they could cure Mildred.

'Of course I'll help your poor friend,' said the captain. 'I'd nearly finished my nap anyway and I need to go down river to pick up some engine parts, so I'm already going that way. If all of you are ready I can take you right away. Just let me get my boat started up.'

He clambered down a hatch and a lot of rattling noises could be heard below. All of a sudden, the engine caught and soon it was pounding away, ready to go.

'It runs on gloopigrape juice,' he explained to Millicent. He pointed to a huge pile of succulent grapes at the rear of the boat, next to a big press for squashing them.

'Could I take a small bunch to give to Mildred when we arrive? She used to love them,' asked Millicent.

'Take all you want,' smiled the captain.

The others clambered aboard and, in a while, they were ready to set off down the peaceful flowing river.

Vera sat at the stern, shading herself with a parasol.

'All this sun is not good for my complexion,' she complained.

Everybody made themselves comfortable and lay back, gazing at the lovely scenery. As they began to slowly leave the jungle with its leafy plants and emerald trees, the sides of the river became steeper and rockier. The water passage narrowed until the purple boat was chugging its way through a steep valley of solid rock. They were going much faster now, because the water was rushing them along.

'I can see why it's called the Rapid River,' remarked Oakum to the captain.

'Oh, it gets much rougher than this,' replied the big hippopotamuddle, pushing his hat to the back of his head.

It did get rougher. Suddenly, the water was splashing noisy white spray against the rocks by the river bank, and the captain was steering very carefully around them. Swampy and Oakum looked alarmed by the speed with which they were rushing past the jagged rocks and realized why the witch hadn't suggested that they come this way. He would never have got his boat up the river against this current.

Sticklenose was wriggling in Willow's arms, clapping his hands enthusiastically at all the splashing. Every time the water pounded against a huge rock, he cheered very loudly. Snagglefang, however, crept underneath his seat and was hiding his head under both of his wings.

'What do we do if we crash?' asked Swampy, nervously.

'Oh, the Captain almost never crashes,' Vera smiled back at Swampy.

'Almost never? Does that mean that sometimes he does?' Oakum worried, but there was too much noise from the white crashing water, and nobody could hear him anymore. He gripped tightly to the rails on the side of the boat.

'Just one more rapid and we're through,' called the captain, as he pointed the boat between two high boulders whilst the water foamed and spat beneath them. They shot through the gap with only inches to spare.

Beyond the rapids, the river widened and the water became much calmer. They left the craggy cliffs behind them and entered a valley filled with smaller rocks and boulders. Soon they were steaming their way down a wide earth-banked river, winding softly through great plains of swaying grass. Every now and then, a solitary willow tree dipped its branches in the water.

'Nearly there, now,' said the captain, pointing at another ramshackle jetty in the distance. As they approached, they could see a faded painted sign. It read 'BEWILDERBOAT JUNCTION'.

The captain slowed down the boat and gently moored it to the wooden platform, so that everyone could disembark. The passengers all thanked the captain before he carried on alone, to get his spare parts.

Swampy and Oakum helped with the mooring ropes and soon the purple boat was cruising away down the great green river.

'We had better get back to your woods quickly,' Vera reminded everyone. 'Which is the right way?'

'I don't know,' worried Willow. 'This place isn't on my map.'

She pulled the map out anyway, just to see if there were any clues that she might have missed.

'Look. Bewilderboat Junction *is* on your map. Just there. So is the Rapid River,' Swampy pointed out, 'and it shows the way home too.'

'I'm sure all that wasn't there before. How odd,' said Willow. Then she remembered it was a map that the witch had given her. Perhaps the map was magical.

They followed its directions across a huge grassy plain studded with a few bushy trees. Every now and then there were little herds of doe-eyed deer grazing peacefully. The deer looked up at the strange group of travellers but did not seem at all alarmed. Sticklenose waved at them excitedly from his sling on Willow's back. But the deer were quite shy and they only allowed Snagglefang to come close. They may have thought he was a bird.

Then Swampy's nose twitched. 'I think I can smell our marshes,' he announced happily. He was so pleased to be near to home that he almost ran towards them. Millicent, however, only seemed to move at one speed, which was quite slowly, so they didn't go any faster than before.

They found the first sedge tussocks and reeds as the sun was beginning to turn a golden colour for the evening. Willow felt so happy to be returning safely that she started singing, and soon everyone joined in. The hippopotamuddle didn't know any of the words, so she kept time with deep 'boom-boom' sounds, while Minty just made up her own words anyway, as Millicent hummed along. The marsh was very easy to walk through, with lots of reeds and bulrushes and it was a very contented band of travellers who emerged at the edge of a great lake.

'I know where we are now. We're at the edge of the Scary Lake. We're almost home,' shouted Swampy.

'I can't wait to see dear old Mildred again,' said Millicent. 'She hasn't met Minty yet. I really hope they will be friends.'

She picked a bunch of wild yellow irises to give Mildred as a present.

Snagglefang announced he was missing his fierce gang of Bewilderbats, and, after hugging Sticklenose, he said his goodbyes and flapped off across the water to join them.

They still had to cross the water, so Oakum assembled his boat. The hippopotamuddle announced that she would swim, as she didn't think she would quite fit in the boat. So she removed her pinafore and neatly folded it. Willow put it in her bag, so that it wouldn't get wet. Then the little flotilla pushed out, across the shining lake.

The Crocklebog Cure.

The arrival of the hippopotamuddle had set the Boggle village into much great excitement. The villagers all worried that the platform might not be strong enough for such a large creature, so all of the tables and chairs for the delayed feast were being carried down the winding stairs to the firmer ground below.

The bunting from the abandoned party was still colourfully decorating the main platform, and the Grubbles had clearly been hard at work, as many of the villagers were sporting smart red socks and other brightly coloured clothes.

Ticklechin welcomed the hippopotamuddle at the entrance to the village, and she was soon surrounded by a huge gang of Boggle children all asking excited questions at the same time. She smiled and showed them all of her mud-cleaning things. Then the smaller Boggles offered everyone great steaming bowls of clunknettle soup.

Once the travellers had drunk their warm soup, Swampy ran off up the staircase to give his mum a huge hug. Oakum was so delighted to see his parents again that he burst into song.

As usual, the witch arrived exactly when she was needed and she was very pleased to see the hippopotamuddle again.

'We'd all better have a look at your sick patient straight away,' suggested Vera.

The witch showed them over to where Mildred was resting on her reed bed.

They could hear Mildred's voice as they approached. '*Ith* that clunknettle *th*oup I *th*mell? I'm very ill, but I could manage one more little bowl,' she was saying.

Then she saw Milicent wearing her blue lace headscarf.

When two crocklebogs are really pleased to see each other there is a lot to be said for standing well back. With their great tails swishing everywhere in pleasure, the sisters gave each other a huge excited hug. Mildred's bed of reeds was scattered over most of the nearby bushes and some of the blankets were now floating in the water.

'You look exactly the same as ever,' exclaimed Milicent, happily.

'But I'm completely pink now,' protested Mildred.

'And a lovely shade of pink too,' said her sister. 'Most fetching.'

When Vera, the hippopotamuddle, managed to get to the invalid's bedside, she found a very pleased Mildred sitting up in bed, drinking clunknettle soup.

'How are you feeling dear?' Vera asked the thorny crockle-bog.

Mildred passed a huge hankie across her brow and explained that she was not feeling too bad, considering everything.

Minty bounced in, with her fluffy wings looking rather be-draggled, as she had forgotten to take them off when she swam across the Scary Lake.

'I want to be that colour, mummy. Pink would suit me,' she

said to her mother. But Millicent was too busy gazing at Mildred to listen.

While the the hippopotamuddle took Mildred's pulse, Millicent chatted to her sister.

'I've brought you some special gloopigrapes. They used to be your favourite fruit,' she said.

Mildred was very pleased and asked for some straight away, but they had gone.

'Oh dear, I've done it again,' said the hippopotamuddle sadly, as she removed a very squashed bunch of grapes from beneath where she had been sitting. Not all of the grapes were completely squashed though. Mildred ate them very slowly, and with great relish.

'We've got you flowers too,' said Minty. 'I know you can't eat them because I've tried, but they look very nice.'

The hippopotamuddle went off for a quick chat with the witch. Then she announced that she had a medicine which would make Mildred feel quite well immediately. She spooned a black oily liquid into Mildred's mouth. The effect was instant. Mildred jumped out of bed and rushed over to the water, which she began drinking fast.

'*Pthoooth! Yeachhy!*' Mildred exclaimed. 'That i*th* even more horrid than pongiporridge.'

But she suddenly found that she felt quite well again, so she thanked Vera most gratefully.

'The good bit about being ill i*th* that people bring you yummy food, but the bad bit i*th* that you don't really want to eat much of it,' she explained.

Vera said that she would need a few minutes to brew a potion from the orange flowers to remove Mildred's pink stain. While it was being prepared, Mildred chatted to her niece, Minty. The two got along immediately.

'I'm a tremendous swimmer and terribly good at diving,' Minty told her aunt.

'I'm learning *th*ynchroni*th*ed *th*wimming,' said Mildred. 'We could do it together if you like.'

They agreed to have a practice just as soon as Mildred was cured of being pink, which in a very short while she was. This time, the potion was rubbed on to her and it turned out to be rather a nicer way to recover.

'Now, we should go and clean all that polluted mud and help

all those poor birds, while there is enough light,' said Vera to the witch.

They said that they wouldn't need any help, but that it would be very nice if the feast could be ready for them when they came back. Then they headed off towards the Long Lagoon in a sturdy Boggle boat, to see what they could do. The hippopotamuddle was carrying an enormous wooden spoon to stir all the mud with.

'At last we can have that party,' the Boggle villagers all said to one another.

Everybody got busily to work, preparing their village for the evening event. Willow and Swampy's mum made even more soup, and Oakum ran over to the Twiggle village to invite them too. Mildred and Minty set off to learn a synchronised swimming routine to perform for everybody as part of the entertainment.

The BeWILDerfeast

When the hippopotamuddle and the witch came back from the Long Lagoon, they looked very pleased and explained that everything was going to be alright.

'I'll need a few days to get the mud completely clean, but it is all quite safe now and the birds are better too,' said Vera, smiling.

Ticklechin announced that the Grubbles would like to sing a Song of Thanks to the hippopotamuddle before the feast began.

The tribe of Grubbles gathered on the edge of the main platform so that Vera and the witch could see them from the grassy clearing below. The other villagers all gathered around them to listen. Once again the gentle rich Grubble voices soared into their melodic tune. It was a beautiful song, and it was just coming to its very quiet and delicate end when there was a sudden noise of splashing and wheezing from the water ponds, by the village.

'Bother! Have we started too soon?' enquired a noisy little voice.

It was Mildred and Minty doing their synchronised swimming routine. The Grubbles cheered when they saw them, and began to sing little ripples of rhythm, which went perfectly with the swimming display.

Mildred swam around in figures of eight, while Minty dived

over and under her tail and, for the grand finale, they both disappeared under water for a long time until Mildred snorted a huge water-spout high into the air. Then they both rose from the water until they were almost balancing on the tips of their tails, as they waggled their wide spread arms in unison. The effect was a bit spoiled when Minty fell over backwards with a huge splash, but the applause from the watching villagers was deafening. Everyone threw roses into the water to show their appreciation.

Then it was time to eat. The mudwort jelly was delicious, the acorn beer was fizzy and, of course, there was lots and lots of sweetsludge pie. There was even some pongiporridge for those who wanted it. Everybody chatted loudly. Most of the Boggles were sporting their bright red socks and Ticklechin explained to anybody who would listen that his were the first ones ever. Swampy told everyone tales about their great adventure, and occasionally, Willow and the other travellers got a few words in. Mildred was clutching a huge bouquet of roses and listening appreciatively.

'You did all that for me? Thank you *th*o much. Perhap*th* Minty and me could make up another *th*wim for you to-morrow, if you like,' she said.

Swampy thought that he would enjoy that very much.

After the feast came the dancing. The Twiggles did their usual scampering whirls about the branches, and the Boggles mostly stood on their heads and waggled their legs in the air. The Grubbles danced together in fours and eights, as they linked arms and twirled each other around. All about their heads fluttered the cheerful wings of the bats as they cavorted above in the sky. Snagglefang and Beaker played a game of throwing little bits of nutbug crunch at each other and catching it in their mouths as they flew.

By the jetty, on the edge of the grassy dancing area, Millicent and the hippopotamuddle linked arms and skipped a very graceful and stately jig as the ground shook softly beneath them. The music grew louder and the dancing became faster. Mildred and Minty decided that it might be more fun to go dancing in the water.

'I don't want any more trouble from my tail flicking about,' explained Mildred. So the two crocklebogs worked out more synchronised swimming moves as they splashed about happily.

Oakum sat down with his mum and dad, to catch his breath.

'It's so lovely to have you here again. I hope you can stay this time. I could fix up the house in the woods where you used to eat your pongiporridge,' he offered.

'Thank you, Oakum, but we really do prefer travelling about,' said Oakum's dad, shaking his head. 'But I'll tell you what. I could come back next year, if you like.'

'Why don't we give a party every year, and then I could always see you,' suggested Oakum. 'I'll ask the witch.'

The witch thought that this was a wonderful idea.

So it was agreed. The Grubbles would visit each summer. Ticklechin was especially delighted as Oakum's dad promised to mend his socks every time.

As the party came to an end, Minty sat on a log and cuddled up to the hippopotamuddle.

'I like this place,' said Minty, contentedly. 'There is always

enough to eat and me and Mildred are going to do lots more synchronised swimming tomorrow.'

She snuggled up in the great grey hippopotamuddle's lap and soon began snoring very quietly.

The
End